STEPHEN  CURRY
I AM EXTRAORDINARY

D1457808

ILLUSTRATED BY
GENEVA BOWERS

Unanimous
Publishing

PENGUIN WORKSHOP

It was the first day at a new school for Zoe. She was a straight-A student who loved soccer. She practiced a lot at home, perfecting her solo skills. All summer, Zoe had dreamed about trying out for the school soccer team.

But for as long as Zoe could remember, she was different. She was no ordinary kid. And all she ever wanted was to be ordinary, just like all the other kids in school.

Her brother, Aaron, tried to reassure her about the new school.

But Zoe wasn't excited. Instead, she was

NERVOUS.

That's because Zoe wore hearing aids to help her hear. She worried that the kids at the new school might not accept her for who she was. And she worried she wasn't good enough to make the team, especially if she couldn't hear as well as the others. These thoughts bounced around her head like balls in a pinball machine.

Zoe wanted to play, but she worried she couldn't keep up.

I THINK I'LL JUST SIT THIS ONE OUT.

Zoe watched as the kids played soccer, wishing that she had the courage and confidence to play with them.

Zoe sat in class and listened to her teacher,
but all she could think about was soccer.

She wanted to try out for the school team, but she knew that on the field, she'd be more comfortable with her hair up. Everyone would be able to see her hearing aids. So, she came up with an idea just before recess.

At first, Zoe could keep up with some of the kids, but she quickly realized it was much more difficult than she thought.

Zoe practiced every day and night that week. Soccer tryouts were held on the big field, and Zoe made the team with ease. In a few weeks, the season began.

On the field, she wore her hearing aids, and Mila wore her protective glasses. Together, the duo was unstoppable. Their team made the playoffs and made it all the way to the championship game.

I AM EXTRAORDINARY!

To all the kids who feel underrated . . .
You are extraordinary—SC

PENGUIN WORKSHOP
An imprint of Penguin Random House LLC, New York

First published in the United States of America by Penguin Workshop,
an imprint of Penguin Random House LLC, New York, 2024

Copyright © 2024 by Unanimous Media Holdings, LLC
Creative Direction by Erick Peyton
Content Editor Kalyna Maria Kutny
Design by Lynn Portnoff

Visit us online at penguinrandomhouse.com.

Library of Congress Cataloging-in-Publication Data is available.

Manufactured in China

ISBN 9780593386064   10 9 8 7 6 5 4 3 2 1 HH